English translation by Rosemary Lanning
Lektorat Brigitte Hanhart Sidjanski
This text has been abridged for the dual language edition · Der Text wurde für die zweisprachige Ausgabe gekürzt.
© 2002 für die englisch/deutsche Ausgabe. © 1998 Nord-Süd Verlag AG, Gossau Zürich und Hamburg
Alle Rechte, auch die der Bearbeitung oder auszugsweisen Vervielfältigung, gleich durch welche Medien, vorbehalten
Lithographie: Photolitho AG, Gossau Zürich ·DTP/Satz: Pro Desk AG, Uster
Gesetzt in der Bauer Bodoni, 16 Punkt · Druck: Proost N.V., Turnhout
ISBN 3 314 01274 8

Die Deutsche Bibliothek – CIP-Einheitsaufnahme
Ein Titelsatz für diese Publikation ist bei der Deutschen Bibliothek erhältlich.

Besuchen Sie uns im Internet: www.nord-sued.com

Hans de Beer

Little Polar Bear
and the Brave Little Hare

Der kleine Eisbär
und der Angsthase

North-South Books · Nord-Süd Verlag

Lars, the little polar bear, had a hill all to himself. He liked to sit there and look out over the ice and snow, as far as the sea. One day he heard a quiet wimpering. He lifted his nose, sniffed and followed the unfamiliar scent.
He soon came to a deep hole. Who could be down there?

Lars, der kleine Eisbär, hatte einen Hügel ganz für sich allein. Da saß er gern und schaute über Eis und Schnee bis zum Meer.
Eines Tages hörte er ein leises Wimmern. Er hielt die Nase hoch, schnupperte und folgte dem fremden Geruch.
Schon bald kam er zu einem tiefen Loch. Wer konnte da unten sein?

Down below sat a little hare, trembling.
"Don't be afraid! I'll help you," said Lars, and he pushed down a whole lot of snow. The littel hare understood immediately and, with a hop, hop, hop, he was soon out of the hole.
"I was so frightened," he murmered,
"But everything is all right now." Lars reassured the trempling hare.

Unten saß zitternd ein kleiner Hase!
»Hab keine Angst! Ich werde dir helfen«, sagte Lars und schubste ganz viel Schnee hinunter. Der kleine Hase begriff schnell und – hopp-hopp-hopp – schon war er oben!
»Ich hatte solche Angst!«, sagte er leise.
»Jetzt ist doch alles wieder gut«, beruhigte Lars den zitternden Hasen.

"I'm Hugo", said the little hare.
"And I'm Lars. Come on, let's have a race!"
Hugo ran the fastest.
Suddenly, it began to snow heavily, and it grew darker and
darker. When Hugo and Lars could hardly see anything any
more they snuggled down in the snow and waited for the sky
to grow light again.
"We'll never find our way back home!"
"Don't worry, Hugo" said Lars. "I have always found my
way home before."

»Ich bin Lena«, sagte der kleine Hase.
»Und ich bin Lars. Komm, lass uns um die Wette rennen!«
Lena war schneller.
Plötzlich fing es heftig an zu schneien und es wurde immer
dunkler. Als Lena und Lars kaum mehr etwas sehen
konnten, kuschelten sie sich in den Schnee und warteten, bis
der Himmel wieder hell wurde.
»Wir finden nie mehr nach Hause!«
»Keine Angst, Lena!«, sagte Lars beruhigend. »Ich habe
noch immer nach Hause gefunden.«

"I'm hungry," moaned Hugo.
Then they heard a loud rattling, and Hugo quickly hid in
the snow.
"What a scaredy-hare you are!" cried Lars, laughing.
"That was only a snowmobile from the polar station. I have
often found delicious things to eat there. I know the way
home from there, too."

»Ich habe Hunger«, jammerte Lena.
Da hörten sie ein lautes Rasseln und Lena versteckte sich
schnell im Schnee.
»Du bist ja ein Angsthase!«, rief Lars und lachte. »Das war
doch nur ein Schneemobil von der Polarstation. Dort habe
ich schon oft leckere Sachen zu essen gefunden! Und von
dort kenne ich den Weg nach Hause.«

"Then let's go home quickly," said Hugo with relief.
"I'm not hungry any more."
"But I am! Come on, scaredy-hare."
They found fish, bread and even two carrots!
"I want to have a look around," said Lars. "You can
wait there on the hill."

»So lass uns schnell nach Hause gehen«, sagte Lena
erleichtert. »Ich habe keinen Hunger mehr.«
»Aber ich! Komm, du kleiner Angsthase.«
Sie fanden Fisch, Brot und sogar zwei Mohrrüben!
»Ich will mich noch ein wenig umsehen«, sagte Lars.
»Du kannst dort auf dem Hügel warten.«

The little polar bear climbed up onto the roof. He heard
strange noises coming out of an opening. Curious, he leand
forward, further and further – and that's when it happened!

Der kleine Eisbär kletterte aufs Dach. Aus einer Öffnung
hörte er seltsame Geräusche. Neugierig beugte er sich vor,
immer weiter – und da passierte es!

Lars tumbled head over heels into the shaft! It was hot, and he was surrounded by winking lights and sinister beeps. Now Lars wished he were home! He tried to slip out through a door and run away. But all the other doors were locked. Lars was very scared.

Lars fiel kopfüber in den Schacht! Es war heiß und um ihn herum piepste und blinkte es unheimlich. Jetzt wäre auch Lars gerne zu Hause gewesen!
Er wollte durch die Türe schlüpfen und hinausrennen. Aber alle Türen nach draußen waren verriegelt. Lars hatte große Angst.

Suddenly Lars heard the snowmobile. In despair he looked around for a hiding place. The man would come in at any moment!
Hugo had heard the snowmobile too. I have got to help Lars! he thought, and he ran down the hill, as fast as lightning.

Plötzlich hörte Lars das Schneemobil. Verzweifelt suchte er nach einem Versteck. Der Mann wird gleich kommen!
Auch Lena hatte das Schneemobil gehört. Ich muss Lars helfen!, dachte sie und rannte blitzschnell hinunter.

Hugo bounded up onto the roof, and shovelled snow into the shaft. Now Lars knew that Hugo was up there. But the man didn't know where the snow was coming from. He went outside to look, leaving the door open. He had not noticed the little polar bear.

In großen Sätzen sprang Lena aufs Dach und schaufelte Schnee in den Schacht. Jetzt wusste Lars, dass Lena da oben war. Aber der Mann wusste nicht, woher der Schnee kam. Er ging hinaus, um nachzusehen, und ließ die Tür offen. Den kleinen Eisbären hatte er nicht bemerkt.

Lars crept out of the door and ran away.
"Come down, Hugo, quickly! Here I am!"
Then Hugo leaped off the roof in one bound,
and dashed between the man's legs.

Lars schlich durch die Tür und rannte davon.
»Komm runter, Lena, schnell! Ich bin hier!«
Da sprang Lena in einem Satz vom Dach und
flitzte dem Mann durch die Beine.

Lars and Hugo were running a reace, and once again Hugo ran fastest.
"Wait for me! I'm scared!"
"But everything is all right now," Hugo reassured the trembling little polar bear. They set off for home together.

Lars und Lena rannten um die Wette. Und wieder war Lena schneller!
»Warte doch auf mich! Ich habe Angst!«
»Jetzt ist doch alles wieder gut«, beruhigte Lena den zitternden Eisbären. Zusammen machten sie sich auf den Heimweg.

Lars and Hugo became good friends. Sometimes they were allowed to spend the night together, too. Then they shovelled snow into a little mound to give them shelter from the icy polar wind. They snuggled down beside the snow mound and happily fell asleep.

Lars und Lena wurden richtige Freunde. Manchmal durften sie auch nachts zusammenbleiben. Dann schaufelten sie den Schnee zu einem kleinen Hügel, um sich vor dem eisigen Polarwind zu schützen. Sie kuschelten sich an den Hügel und schliefen zufrieden ein.